Dark Matter

by

Genieve Dawkins

Dark Matter

By

Genieve Dawkins

Published by Genieve Dawkins, Lulu Edition

ISBN: 978-1-300-06788-7

Apocalypse Now

1 And I saw when the Lamb opened one of the
seals, and I heard, as it were the noise of
thunder, one of the four beasts saying, Come
and see.
2 And I saw, and behold a white horse: and he
that sat on him had a bow; and a crown was
given unto him: and he went forth conquering,
and to conquer.
3 And when he had opened the second seal, I
heard the second beast say, Come and see.
4 And there went out another horse *that
was* RED: and *power* was given to him that
sat thereon to take peace from the earth, and
that they should kill one another: and there
was given unto him a great sword.
5 And when he had opened the third seal, I
heard the third beast say, Come and see. And I
beheld, and lo a black horse; and he that sat on
him had a pair of balances in his hand.
6 And I heard a voice in the midst of the four
beasts say, A measure of wheat for a penny,
and three measures of barley for a penny;
and *see* thou hurt not the oil and the wine.
7 And when he had opened the fourth seal, I
heard the voice of the fourth beast say, Come
and see.
8 And I looked, and behold a pale horse: and his
name that sat on him was Death, and Hell

followed with him. And power was given unto them over the fourth part of the earth, to kill with sword, and with hunger, and with death, and with the beasts of the earth.

6 And in those days shall men seek death, and shall not find it; and shall desire to die, and death shall flee from them.

20 Wherefore is light given to him that is in misery, and life unto the bitter *in* soul;

21 which long for death, but it *cometh* not; and dig for it more than for hid treasures;

22 which rejoice exceedingly, *and* are glad, when they can find the grave?

23 *Why is light given* to a man whose way is hid, and whom God hath hedged in?

24 For my sighing cometh before I eat, and my

roarings are poured out like the waters.

25 For the thing which I greatly feared is come
upon me, and that which I was afraid of is
come unto me.

26 I was not in safety, neither had I rest, neither
was I quiet; yet trouble came.

The Aftermath

There was a dull orange-red glow everywhere. It had been there at the back of Angelo's eyelids when he had first become aware. He opened his eyes with a great effort, only to be greeted by the same dull orange-red atmosphere. He could not escape it. He could feel the dull orange-red warmth in his stomach and could taste it in his mouth and in the back of his throat. It choked his nostrils and pressed softly against his open eyeballs. He blinked.

It was still there.

Angelo moved his arm through the soupy orange-red atmosphere and pinched himself. A sharp pain shot through his forearm and jerked his brain back into full awareness. Memory came rushing back.

He gasped.

What had he done?

"No!" he screamed. His breath punched back the orange-red dullness as it blasted out of his lungs. The orange-red atmosphere rolled back into his mouth with a strange, soupy persistence. It swallowed the sound of his scream with a delirious vengeance.

"No," Angelo whispered again. The sound now came out as nothing but a small, choked sob in the back of his throat.

"Pierre!" he screamed. The words bounced into the orange-red soup, wavered in a ghostly echo and then were swallowed up by the soup, as if they had never been.

Angelo stumbled forward into the red nothing. He needed to find someone, anyone. He needed to explain. He needed to fix this.

He pressed through the soup, screaming for help, shouting for Pierre. He ran on like this for hours, finding nothing but the dense, orange-red soup. It was above him, and below, it enveloped him like a never-ending cocoon. He ran till he could run no more, then he rested for a moment. Revived, he walked until he could walk no more. Till at long last, Angelo fell on his face and started to crawl. He crawled and he cried, and he sobbed and he crawled, but there was no end to this misery. There was nothing anywhere but soup.

Angelo lay there in a crumpled heap and cried. He understood. A silent tear rolled down his cheek. He knew.

A Man So Ordinary

"Whoa there!" the man in the expensive suit yelled, as he ducked out of the way of Angelo's serving tray. Angelo looked around, trying to determine what Expensive-Suit's problem was. As he did so, he forgot all about the tray full of fancy red fruit drinks he was carrying. The stress of trying to remember who had ordered what and which tables had requested drinks was beginning to get to him. The noise, heat, loud music and atmosphere had triggered a pounding headache, but he was here and had to work because he needed the money. The guy in the expensive leather suit jumped out of the way of his serving tray, narrowly avoiding an accident. As Angelo twisted his head around to get a closer look at the man, the motion sent a bolt of pain up the back of his head. He lost his focus for a moment as the pain passed, but it was just long enough to unbalance the tray. He barely registered the sound of the woman screaming as glass after glass of ice and cold fruit juice fell off Angelo's tray into her hair, down her breasts and spattered bright red splashes all over her expensive, white designer dress.

The noise of her shrill screams finally penetrated through Angelo's pain haze. He looked at her in shocked horror, with his mouth wide open. He looked like a slack-jawed idiot, standing there holding the tray and gaping while the woman tried to brush crushed ice, fruit and little paper umbrellas from her matted hair and ruined clothes. Angelo's floor manager rushed over. She cast Angelo a look of complete murderous rage and hastily started apologizing to the woman.

"It's ruined!" the woman screamed. Her mascara ran down her red fruit-juice-stained face. Her hair hung in matted clumps, with bits of strawberry, pineapple, lime and lemon stuck in it here and there. Misery and her loud screaming contorted her face into an ugly mask of anger. Angelo stared at her dumbly. He thought she looked like some kind of grotesque clown. He wasn't particularly fond of clowns.

His manager shot him a glare of unadulterated scorn and hatred. Angelo suddenly felt small. He looked at the grotesque clown and stammered. "I'm...uh, I'm so sorry," he offered, automatically reaching for the soaked napkins on his tray. He grabbed a handful of semi-dry ones and used them in a clumsy attempt to mop the mess off the front of the woman's dress.

He was further flustered when this angered her even more.

"Leave me alone, you stupid oaf!" she screamed angrily at the top of her lungs. Her voice came out in a tinny, whiny timbre that caused everyone at the party to cease their conversations and shift their attention to the spectacle unfolding at Angelo's station.

"I'm really so sorry," Angelo stammered again. The soggy, limp clump of napkins dangled awkwardly from his fingers. He looked at it forlornly, like all his sadness could be poured into the simple, soaked object.

"Angelo, why don't you pick up those glasses and take them back to the kitchen?" his manager interjected in a high-pitched, stressed-out voice, eager to get the situation under control.

Angelo nodded dumbly, bent down, retrieved the glasses from the around the woman's ankles and balanced them precariously on the tray.

He was in the middle of this occupation when something sharp hit him in the ribs, sending pain shooting up and down his torso.

"Ow!" Angelo screamed, and the glasses toppled off the tray, crashing to the ground with a loud, splintering sound as he instinctively dropped the tray and grabbed hold of his hurting side. He looked up, to see the woman glaring wickedly down at him, her grotesque clown-face with its smeared makeup and runny mascara boring a hole in his skull. A similar pain spread through his right buttock as she landed another swift kick to his derriere, using the point of her triangular-fronted heels to deadly effect.

She twisted her nasty red mouth into a sneer, "That'll teach you, you dumb waiter," she said snidely, shaking the ankle with the pointed stiletto heel that she had used to kick Angelo. He looked at her, her face a mask of ugly, sneering snobbery, and thought for a moment that the ruined makeup and soaked dress suited her ugly personality. He suddenly no longer cared and he no longer felt sorry.

An uproar of laughter went up around the venue, as guests whispered to their friends that the clown had kicked the waiter. Angelo's ears roared and his face burned.

He hurriedly shoveled the glasses unto the tray, heedless of the splinters that cut into his hands, causing little dots of blood to spring forward.

He walked out of the room with a sure, confident, angry stride, without a second look back at the clown-woman or his hissing manager.

"Stupid, dumb waiter," the woman sneered as he walked past her. Her friends snickered.

Angelo stalked straight into the kitchen, ignoring the questions from the rest of the serving staff and the chefs. He dumped the lot, glasses, silver serving tray, straws, napkins and all into the nearest bin, ignoring the loud "Ois!" from the floor manager.

He wiped blood and glass splinters down the front of his pants, walked to the locker room, opened his locker and retrieved his things.

The cold air blasted in his face and blew his hair out into a puffy frame. His eyes were empty, blank.

Angelo stepped out into the night.

Thwarted

"So, Mr. Bixio, I see here that you hold a Bachelor of Science degree in Computer Science," the hiring manager intoned, frowning importantly.

"And Chemistry," Angelo added helpfully. "I did two majors at undergraduate level."

"That is an odd combination. How did you come by such a combination of unrelated subjects?"

"Well, I've always had a keen interest in science," Angelo responded, wistfully. His facial features softened as his mind hearkened back to his days as a carefree undergraduate student. He had been surprisingly brilliant, with an aptitude for the physical sciences. He had spent most of his four years as an undergraduate on his feet, in one kind of laboratory or the other.

Misfortune had struck somehow, and his brilliance had not shown itself in his examination results. He had come from very humble beginnings, with no rungs on the all-important social ladder. He had been unable to obtain any jobs suited to his intellectual level, and had no money to start his own business. He had settled into whatever positions he had been able to secure, squirreling away what little he could from his meager earnings after his bills were paid. Slowly, he had been able to save enough to go to graduate school while working, and had managed to scrimp out a Master of Science degree in Information Technology while working sixteen-hour days.

His simple looks and humble demeanor belied his mental capabilities. Unfortunately for him, employers were always willing to look beyond his qualifications and experience, and were content to only see his small size, soft voice and humble demeanor, and so would quickly dismiss him as unimportant, assume he was unintelligent and treat him poorly. He never complained.

Angelo was a quiet, calm soul on the surface. One can never tell what monsters swim beneath the calm surface of a deep blue sea.

Two hours and several assessments later, Angelo was tired and worn out. He felt the beginnings of another tension headache frisson over the front of his skull.

"We'll let you know. Thanks for coming," the hiring manager said, proffering Angelo his soft, damp palm for a limp, lifeless handshake. An improper thought tried to make its way into

Angelo's aching brain, but he swiftly forced it away. He made a mental effort to appear pleasant and forced a manageably pleasant smile.

Red

The contract was terrible. They were offering him minimum wage to perform some incredibly technical research, article writing and scientific editing of research papers. It was grunt work, and they were clearly taking great advantage of the fact that he was unemployed. For a brief moment, Angelo thought of going back to waiting tables. As he did so, he felt a twinge of pain in his left buttock. He winced. He glanced down at the red letters on the rest of the envelopes in the pile of mail on his lap. "FINAL NOTICE!!!" they screamed at him, threatening all manner of evil in RED. For some reason, the senders of such mail seemed to think that RED caps meant something special. Maybe RED was more special than BLACK or BLUE?? It certainly seemed to have an effect on the postman, who would carefully fold the envelopes so the RED lettering would not show when the mail was delivered. Angelo chuckled softly to himself. He wished he could give the postman a nice Christmas bonus in his traditional envelope, but he had barely enough to buy food, and he was overdrawn, so the poor postman was unlikely to get anything this year, despite his efforts at discretion. All the RED letters in the world couldn't change that. Not even RED could squeeze blood out of a stone.

Angelo looked down at the RED letters and then looked at the exploitative contract. He sighed. He rustled about in his pocket until he found a pen. As he scrawled his signature on the contract, he felt a pang of regret that the ink in the pen was black, not RED.

Begin Edit

The stack of papers fell on the tiny desk with a loud thud. The flimsy little desk seemed alarmingly in danger of buckling under the weight.

Marjorie cleared her throat loudly and wetly. Something huge seemed to be stuck down there. She hawked it up and swallowed. A pleased smile played across her wide, unattractive face. Her thin lips were dry and slightly cracked. Angelo could see gobs of dried mucous in the corners of her eyes. He suppressed a grimace. Appearing nonchalant required a significant amount of mental effort on his part.

"Here. This will get you started," Marjorie croaked. Her deep baritone tones reverberated in Angelo's head. He watched with a morbid fascination as the baritone caused the long, thick, stiff hairs on her chin to quiver delicately. It was an unexpected thing, this graceful, delicate motion on the surface of a woman who was anything but. The incongruity struck a chord somewhere deep in Angelo’s brain and a thought stirred. She caught him looking at her and smiled with a strangely sweet serenity. There was a cold glint in her eyes that belied the serenity of that smile. Angelo felt a twinge of something unfamiliar in his stomach. For a moment, he thought it might be the warning sign of the beginning of a diarrheal episode, but with a dawning awareness, he realized that it was fear. It was some kind of primal warning being sent to his brain by his adrenal system, through the conduit of his innards.

"Yeah," Marjorie drawled. "This lot of How-To articles needs to be written by the end of this week."
She nodded in the direction of the ancient, yellowing computer and tower on the desk. "That computer is your workstation. It's connected to the Internet. You need to do all the research, write the articles, format them according to the guidelines and provide the references for the editor. Every point you make needs to have an online reference. We don't want any original work. Make sure someone has already written it. Oh yeah, we will terminate your contract for any plagiarism. We check."

Angelo gave her a quizzical look, which she ignored.

"Yeah, you also need to find a royalty-free image for every article and add a caption," she continued nonchalantly.

"You need to meet your daily quota and get every article signed off by your assigned editor, which is me," she grinned, showing him her wide, brown teeth.
"If I decide I like your work, you will get paid for the article; otherwise, no money for you." She chuckled dryly, clearly amused by her own personal joke. Angelo didn't see the humor, but managed to grimace up something that resembled a smile.

"Yeah, sugar," Marjorie crooned, "Keep me happy and I might just make sure you get some pay. Now get to work. Time's a-wasting."

As Marjorie waddled off, Angelo picked up the first two documents on the top of the pile. He was surprised by the topics: "How to Install a Thingamjingabobbit" and "How to Solve All the Known Problems in the Universe." He sighed. He had a long, arduous day ahead. His head started pounding as the old, familiar pain returned.

Sunlight streamed through the window and played on Angelo's face. He moaned, groaned and rolled over, shoving his face down into the pillow as he did so, instinctively trying to block out the light.

The alarm on the cell phone he kept beneath the covers on the bed went off. It was a shrill, annoying, insistent sound. Angelo lifted a heavy hand and tried to stop it, but the noise would not be silenced. He turned over, with a loud sigh. He cracked open his eyes and the sunlight seized the opportunity to dance a frenzied dance on his eyelids, temporarily blinding him in the process. Angelo was forced awake as the combination of noise from the alarm and morning sunlight won the Battle of the Bed. He sat upright and searched for the phone under the covers, mumbling to himself as he searched.

He found the phone, shut off the alarm and looked at the time. It was 6 AM on a Saturday morning, but he felt a sudden urgency to get up. His mind was still fuzzy with the last traces of sleep, and he could not quite recall what he needed to do. He knew it must have been important for him to set an alarm for a Saturday morning. He closed his eyes and whispered a prayer of thanks, feeling grateful to be up at all. As the sleep haze cleared, he remembered. He sprang out of bed and ran directly to his living room, looking for his computer. His head ached a little, and he felt the need for a cup of coffee, but it would have to wait. Marjorie had insisted that she wanted all his assigned articles submitted by 6:30 AM on this Saturday morning. He had spent at least 18 hours each day all week doing research, composing, assembling and writing articles. He had been up till 3 AM double-checking everything. Now, he needed to push all the articles into the company's FTP system, which was notoriously slow. No, there was no time for coffee, or even tooth brushing this morning. Angelo sighed and punched the "ON" switch on his laptop. The words on the screen sprang to life and wavered giddily as he tried to focus.

"So," Marjorie droned, draping the folds of her soft body over the edge of Angelo's little desk and shooting him a strangely lecherous look that was more of a frightening grimace than the "come hither" look she had hoped to portray.

She lifted the palm of one hand in the direction of the window and examined the designs on her intricately manicured nails. Angelo looked down and was struck by the incongruity of her delicate, expensive five-inch stilettos and the huge feet and cankles that threatened to suffocate them. He was puzzling over the marvel of engineering that stopped them breaking under her mass when she finally continued.

"Yeah, soooo," she drawled. "What are you doing this weekend?"
Angelo looked up at her and shrugged. He was in no particular mood to discuss his plans to shovel his way through whatever pile of assignments she was planning to drop on him this weekend.

"Would you like to go out to dinner, you know, with me?" she drawled, still examining her nails.

Angelo didn't get the implication and the strangeness of the request threw him off-kilter.

"Well, uh, uh," he stammered, struggling to find the words to get him out of this tricky situation.

"Well, uh, I mean, I can't. I'm sorry," he finally mustered. "I'm spending the weekend with my girlfriend, so I wouldn't be able to make it. I'm really sorry."

The fragile little desk shook and trembled as Marjorie flew off it. Her face was flushed and her grimace of a smile was now wider, broader and much darker. Her stilettos groaned audibly under the sudden pressure, but remarkably, held true.

She stormed past him without another word, over to Matt's desk. Matt was younger than Angelo, new and eager to please. He was also incredibly ambitious and willing to do anything to get ahead. Marjorie fixed her grimace on Matt, who beamed up at her and nodded his assent.

"Good boy. You know how to get ahead in this business," Marjorie crowed. She waddled back to her office, shooting Angelo a dark look of pure hate as she passed his desk. Angelo looked over at Matt. Matt smiled smugly and shot Angelo a dirty look. Angelo sighed and tried to concentrate on the pile of work in his inbox.

Angelo found himself summoned into Marjorie's little office a few hours later. She had squeezed her bulk into a heroic executive chair and was now facing him from behind her cluttered desk.

"How can this be?!"Angelo asked incredulously. His lower lip trembled with a barely concealed anger.

"Well, you don't get paid unless your articles are approved," Marjorie hissed. "And I didn't approve the articles, so no pay for you sweetie. I'm sorry." She smiled a snarky smile that belied her claim of being sorry. Her eyes glinted with an evil iciness.

"But, but I worked on these for two weeks! I have bills to pay!" Angelo shouted.

"Well, those are the breaks," Marjorie said dryly.

Just then, Matt wandered into the office, mincing and prancing with a practiced delicacy. Marjorie smiled at him and he smiled back.

"Why don't you get back to work Angelo," she said, smiling suggestively at Matt and fingering the beads of her necklace. "You're on Scientific Editing detail now. Some Nuclear Physics papers have come in and they're in non-native English. You better get a move on, because you need to edit them to polished perfection by tonight, and they're ten thousand words each."

Angelo sighed.

Basic Nuclear Physics

The loud whine came again. It was even more high-pitched and annoying than the last. It was followed by another, of a different pitch and intensity, and yet another.

Angelo started awake. He was momentarily confused by the noise. It sounded like he was being attacked by a swarm of mosquitoes, but there were no mosquitoes to be seen.

He reached across the desk and flicked on the lamp. The monitor of his laptop flashed on, goaded out of hibernation by the sudden movement. Angelo felt something damp on his arm, where his head had been nestled while he slept at the desk in front of the computer. He looked down. His drawn face and sleep-deprived eyes reflected wetly back from the pool of drool that ran from his arm on to the surface of the desk. He looked at his distorted drool-reflection with dismay as the loud whining sound made its presence known once again.

As the fog cleared from Angelo's brain, he realized that the sound was coming from his lungs. He was wheezing again. He sighed and reached across his desk for his inhaler, knocking papers all over the room in the process. One of the papers caught his eye. The title read ".... Antimatter..." The rest of the title was obscured by the assorted garbage and other occupants of Angelo's desk. He sighed again, put the nozzle of the inhaler in his mouth, pressed down and inhaled sharply.

The whining noise stopped. The room went silent.

"Basic Nuclear Physics." The title blinked on the screen over and over again. Angelo plonked the steaming cup of coffee down on the desk, pulled the laptop closer so he could see and adjusted the glasses on his nose.

"All matter is made up of atoms. Atoms consist of a nucleus and a charged cloud of electrons. The nucleus contains charged protons."

Angelo caught himself snoring as he nodded off to sleep again. He shook himself awake and took a big gulp of the hot coffee.

"Aarrghh! Arrgghh!" he screamed as the scalding liquid burned a layer of skin off his soft palette. He ran to the kitchen for a sip of cool water to cool the burning in his mouth. Now fully awake, he went back to his seat and resumed reading.

The night dragged on and became the wee hours of morning as Angelo alternated between editing papers and learning his basic Nuclear Physics. He read on with a rapt fascination as the details of the relationships between protons and electrons became clear to him. He was amazed by the number of different possibilities of matter in the universe.

"Atoms decay, producing electrons, protons and the much smaller particles of which they are made," the text informed him. Angelo nodded somberly. That made sense. Everything decays. Why should the tiniest components of matter be any different?

"Hmmm," Angelo mused. "So, the atoms decompose over time to release subatomic particles. The subatomic particles themselves can be made to release even smaller particles. As they decompose, they emit radiation. The sum of the masses of the lambda rays that make up the radiation plus the masses of the decomposed particles should be equal to the mass of the initial atom."

It was all very interesting. He saw it now, as through a glass, darkly. It was there, and slowly becoming clear to him. The wonders of the things we cannot see. The very essence of our beings, was being unraveled in front of his eyes. He wondered at the greatness, the brilliance, the grand master design behind it all. It was all so complex, and yet somehow seemed so *purposeful*. There was more to it than just a bunch of interrelated particles. He could feel it in his bones.

"Ah, Einstein's golden rule," Angelo said, delighted to finally come across the world's most well-known piece of human wisdom at last. "$E=mc^2$." The conversion of matter into energy. The mass of matter multiplied by the speed of light squared gives the amount of energy contained in the matter. Matter is technically frozen energy. To release energy from matter, you must combine it with an equivalent amount of antimatter."

Angelo paused. There was that word again. Antimatter. He had seen something about it in one of the papers he had been editing earlier. He tried to recall which of the papers it had been, but was too focused on his reading to really pay any attention to that now.

The law of conservation of energy ran through his mind like a runaway train on a track,

"Energy cannot be created nor destroyed, but is simply converted from one form to another." The conservation of matter energy was slightly different though. Antimatter. Like matter, but with an opposite charge. The thought made him inexplicably uneasy. He felt a small shiver run up his spine. The word felt slightly strange in his mouth. It made his tongue feel fuzzy and left a slightly *ecru t*aste in his mouth. He laughed at that. The thought that a word could taste of a color. The very idea of a color having a taste. If anything antimatter wouldn't taste ecru. It would taste of something darker or of something more passionate, like *RED*, or orange.

"Matter is an incredibly concentrated form of energy. We have not yet been able to release all of the energy from matter."

"All things are composed of matter. Matter is immortal."

"We are made of matter," Angelo thought out loud. "But we are not essentially immortal, are we? Or are we?"

"Where does life fit into the equation? I see energy. I see matter. Where is that elusive thing called life?"

He thought about it for a moment. There was some small slip of logic that he tried to grasp, but his fatigued mind could not hold on to the thought in the early hours of morning.

"Matter and antimatter are created at the same time," Angelo read on. "Particles cannot be created without antiparticles and antiparticles cannot be created without particles," the text proclaimed. "But wait; there is very little antimatter observable in the universe."

"Where did the antimatter go?" Angelo asked, looking out beyond the dim circle of light cast by his desk lamp. His eyes focused on the darkness just beyond the reach of the small circle of light.

"Where did the antimatter go?"

The Interview

"Please, can you try Mr. Ridley's desk again?" Angelo pleaded with the harried looking young receptionist. She cast him an apathetic look from over the big, wide glossy desk in the huge, spacious waiting room of the building. Everything gleamed with a cold chrome-and-glass efficiency. The look the receptionist gave Angelo fit nicely with the cold, unwelcoming atmosphere of the place. The phone buzzed incessantly, with the muted tones of a sound suppressed by too-tiny speakers. Angelo tapped his heel anxiously on the floor. The crisp newness of his smart leather business loafers pinched his heel a little. The stiff, starched business suit was uncomfortable. He tugged at his tie nervously. He felt hot. His head was heavy and stuffy. The rush from the train station to make it to the interview on time had not agreed with the heavy wool of the business suit, and his armpits were beginning to grow damp, in spite of his expensive forty eight hour antiperspirant deodorant and its broken promise of long-lasting dryness. Angelo looked at his palms. They were damp. He didn't want damp palms making the wrong impression on his interviewer. He couldn't stand for anything to go wrong.

He needed this job. The demand letters were piling up rapidly. He could hardly keep his phone on anymore during the daytime because of creditor calls and had taken to simply keeping it on silent. He had no money to pay any bills. He had worked day and night, like a dog, editing documents and turning out articles. Marjorie had resisted him at every turn, finding a never-ending stream of faults with his work to prevent him getting paid. She would insist on a comma and return the work for a rewrite and then reject the work because the newly added comma was out of place. Angelo had tried filing an appeal, but that had just made his tenuous situation worse, as is the situation with some jobs. He had dared to ask a question, so now he was a troublemaker and needed to spend his days walking on eggshells.

Marjorie had not let up on him either. She would smile at him at his desk, or brush against him when she was finding fault with his work. Always just a little too close for comfort. She had been getting bolder. Yesterday, she had pressed her full, heaving bosom into his back while he was standing at his desk going over edits. She hadn't even bothered to hide her intentions. Matt had glared at him with dark hate in his eyes. Angelo suspected that Marjorie had tired of her toy boy and was looking for a new challenge. His resistance seemed to be making her more vindictive and determined, but the thought of compliance was too terrible a thing for his mind to even contemplate. One way or the other, he was in hell.

"You must be Angelo," the fat, rotund, red-faced little man said, as he huffed and puffed and waddled towards the spot at which Angelo stood. Angelo felt a pang of concern. The little man had clearly spent much too much of his life sitting at a desk and the stress of walking down the stairs showed on him. He was sweaty and looked hot, and there was a pulsing green vein just barely visible beneath the thin, sunless skin of his forehead.

"Sorry I'm late," he huffed and puffed and panted, but still managed to say it in the kind of condescending tone that suggested he wasn't sorry at all. "I had some important matters to attend to." Again, there was the slight hint of condescension.

"Not a problem at all sir," Angelo replied, perking up and picking up his briefcase.

"Yes," Ridley said, in a disinterested drawl. "Well, I'm Reginald Archibald Ridley, as your agent should have informed you. If you will please follow me, we can begin the interview. My project manager, Don Assby, will be meeting us in the meeting room to administer the tests and assist with the interview."

Angelo need not have worried about his damp palms after all, as no handshake was proffered.

Ridley led Angelo through a seemingly interminable maze of passages and doors. People were crammed into little workstations everywhere. They glanced at Angelo furtively, with a kind of masked curiosity, but kept working. The place was cold, clinical, full of humans but somehow devoid of humanity. It was cold. Angelo looked around at the workers toiling away in their open plan workstations, hunched over glaring computer screens, typing away. Each one seemed lost in his own barren universe. He was struck by how shabby and somehow unhealthy they all seemed. The modern white collar worker cum wage slave, spending all day in a cramped position, working unpaid overtime, nights, weekends. Used up, stressed out, and yet somehow shabby and droopy rather than enriched and blooming. What were they toiling for, exactly?

A little shiver ran up Angelo's spine. He shook the thoughts from his head and forced himself to focus as Ridley finally found the interview room.
This room was opulent and pristine, in sharp contrast to the cluttered workstations where the busy workers, invisible from here, whiled their days away.

Assby walked in and nodded at Angelo curtly. He slapped the test papers down and barked out the instructions. He and Ridley walked away, leaving Angelo to the task. Angelo peered intently at the papers, picked up his pen and started feverishly scribbling away.

They grilled him for hours, tossing question after question at him with the rapidity of machine-gunfire. Angelo kept calm and paced himself, fully answering everything they threw at him. He had spent many hours preparing for the interview and had done so many interviews and answered so many questions over the course of time that they could not faze him. They were determined to try. The interview dragged on. He talked until he was hoarse. He had to beg for a glass of water, as they had not even thought of offering him the customary beverage.

As the evening faded into the grey tones of dusk,

Assby gave him a weak, limp handshake and bid him farewell. Ridley escorted him down the maze of passages and back out of the building. He proffered Angelo a limp, soggy hand to shake and a weak, non-committal, "Thank you for coming. We'll be in touch," while deftly avoiding eye contact. He then turned brusquely on his heel and walked away.

Angelo felt the familiar sinking feeling in the pit of his stomach. He hadn't eaten for hours. His stomach wanted to be hungry, but he remembered that he had had to forfeit any work and earnings for the day to attend the interview, so he wouldn't be able to buy anything to eat anyway. He felt around in his pocket for bus fare.

As if on cue, a raggedy beggar with the characteristic white crust of hunger on his lips and a deep, painful hunger in his eyes came up to Angelo.

"Please sir, I'm hungry. Please give me money to buy food, even just a cup of coffee," he said, extending a dirty hand covered in sores. Angelo thought of the bus fare in his pocket and remembered that he had not been able to afford a cup of coffee in so long, he couldn't even recall the last time he'd set foot in a fast food joint. He looked at the piteous creature, bent from care and worry and saw himself, except he had not totally given up on life or faith. God had better plans in store for him. He knew it for sure. His stomach came back to life as his thought processes calmed down. A pang of hunger struck him just them. He reached into his pocket for the last of the money. It was nothing but a few coins. They jingled gaily as they fell into the beggar's dirty palm.

"Thank you so much, kind sir," the beggar said, sounding truly grateful. Angelo forced a half-smile.

A bus cruised past, temporarily blocking out the dim light of the slowly setting sun as Angelo trudged off alone on the sidewalk. It would be a long two-hour walk home and it was cold, so very cold.

In the opulent, pristine glass tower, Assby looked at Ridley with contempt. His upper lip trembled as he sneered. He tossed Angelo's test papers on the reject pile.

"Yes, I know he had the best results," he hissed, "but you know *they* can never be as senior as one of our own people. Those kinds of people cannot be allowed into these kinds of jobs. What would people say?"

He looked at Ridley with open disdain.

"Yes," Ridley agreed, feeling a little like Pilate felt when he washed the blood from his hands, "Yes, they are always junior. You know their educational systems are inferior to ours. The young man we saw before him is one of us; he would be a better fit to our team."

"Hmmm," Assby snorted as he tossed the rest of Angelo's assessment papers in the reject pile.

"Notify his agency, will you? And clean up in here. I have a date."

The News

His agent called on Monday morning to tell him the news. He had outperformed the others on all the standard assessments, but the managers felt that another candidate was the "perfect fit" for this job and had "more experience." How much more? Well he had all of five years experience in comparison to Angelo's ten, but he was a better fit with "more relevant experience." Angelo was told they were sorry and wished him the best in his future endeavors. Yeah, right.

He thanked the agent and sent out the usual round of "thank you" emails with a heavy heart. His mood soon lightened, however, as his phone loudly announced, "INCOMING MESSAGE!" multiple times with its mechanical, robotic, triumphant insistence.

Angelo pressed the buttons on the phone and smiled. His smile was beautiful, like a sliver of sunshine from behind a thundercloud. It broke through his misery and lit up his entire persona.

It was from his girlfriend, Jill. He had not heard from her in days and he'd been so busy preparing for the interview and struggling with his editing that he hadn't been able to get in touch with her. The message made him so happy. She wanted to see him tonight, after she had finished work. His heart sang. He could taste the soft, sweet kiss of her lips and hear the melodious tones of her laugh already. Jill was his sunshine. He loved her with a fervent love that knew no bounds and was like nothing he had ever felt before. He was in awe of her love and grateful to her for standing with him through these incredibly rough times. She had been there for him, full of love and support in those first dark days. He desperately wanted his life to get back on track so he could propose to her and maybe have the pleasure of her in his life forever.

Yes, in this life, everything could go wrong, but sweet Jill, his beloved Jill, made it all worthwhile.

He picked out his most flattering clothes to wear today and went on his way to work with a soft smile in his eyes and on his lips.

Marjorie was in an especially foul mood, and his special outfit and extra care with his grooming routine did nothing to help. Her eyes brightened, lit from within by some evil furnace, when he walked through the door, with that secret smile playing on his lips. She scanned him quickly, drinking in every inch of his person, assessing him and discovering his hidden secrets. Jealousy flared in her like a consuming fire. Her world was a white-hot green.

There he was, grinning, beaming and looking smug and self-satisfied. She could almost smell the woman on him. She could sense the stifling, sickly-sweet perfume of that other. She could see inside his mind and the imagery made her physically ill. She could see his thoughts. She saw twisting, writhing, moaning bodies, slick with sweat and hot with pent-up youthful desire. She could see the gleaming tresses, soft, smooth skin and perfect teeth of some young woman there on Angelo's mind. Some woman he loved, who had banished all thoughts of her from his mind.

Marjorie felt vengeance work its way up from her loins. It shot into her belly and made her knees go weak. It grew hotter and wilder as it crept up her torso, into her neck. It flushed her face, suffused with heat. It crept into her eyes and rushed up into her brain, mercifully blocking out the images being projected from his mind into hers. The moaning, the writhing, the sweat, the lust, the brilliant smile, the annoying joy and longing in his face. She needed to wipe the joy out of his life. She needed to blot the memory of that other from his mind, like the moon eclipsing the light of the sun. Rage soared through her like a living thing. It was incredible. Every fiber of her being was alive. She felt turned on, plugged in, connected and powerful. She saw that smile again. The light played on his brilliant white teeth. The light of his joy was too much for her to bear. It fueled her rage like a splash of gasoline on a raging inferno. She unclenched her fists, releasing little droplets of bright red blood where, unknown to her, her nails had been digging into her palms. She lashed out, leapt on Angelo and ripped the smile off his face.

The End of Everything

Angelo didn't know what hit him. He had barely had time to register the fact that Marjorie had jumped on him. His face burned. He tried to see, but everything was RED. He could feel sticky liquid running down his face and he knew everything was wrong, very, very wrong. He needed to escape, to run. He needed to get out of here and get help NOW! He shoved an incredibly heavy mass off his chest, not realizing or caring that it was Marjorie, who was still viciously pounding on him. His lungs were on fire. The loud sound of a swarm of mosquitoes was back again. He could hear them every time he tried to fill his lungs with air.

He dragged himself to his feet and ran blindly. He couldn't see where he was going and he didn't care. He needed to get away. He needed to be anywhere but here.

Angelo was unaware of the spectacle he caused as he ran blindly from the Scientific Editing department of the University. The ripped flesh of his face flapped in the wind as he ran. Blood poured down his face, into his eyes and mouth. His crisp, white shirt was spattered and soaked with blood. Blood ran down his jeans and down into his shoes.

The security guard standing at the entrance to the building next door to his watched in shocked horror as this bloodied spectacle stumbled blindly through the doors, followed by a shouting crowd of shocked spectators. The scientist standing at the door to the physics laboratories paused after doing his retina scan, unaware that the door to the restricted access area had just swung open. He tumbled forward into the lab housing the particle collider as the bloody mess formerly known as Angelo hit him. The door hissed shut behind them before he could quite grasp what had happened.

"Oh my God!" he squealed. He fought against the blind panic that rose in his chest and tried to assess the situation. The security guard was beating against the locked door to the particle laboratory, demanding to know if he was okay. There was a muted din through the door as the babble of spectators from all over the university campus gathered in the room beyond, all trying to figure out what was happening and trying to get help. Someone shoved the security guard away from the glass panels in the door and the crowd surged forward, fighting to get a good view. The physicist felt something sticky on his hands and looked down. It was blood. The man had got blood all over him and was now struggling to speak.

He knelt down and performed a quick assessment of the extent of Angelo's injuries. "It's going to be alright," he said to Angelo, trying to reassure him. "I'm Pierre. I'm a nuclear physicist and you're in my lab. I'll get you help. Just don't try to move."

Pierre released Angelo, who was wheezing alarmingly, gasping for air and starting to turn blue beneath the blood, wiped the blood from his hands down the front of his pristine white lab coat and made his way to the wall-mounted emergency intercom. There were no phones in the laboratory, as the frequencies interfered with the delicate laboratory equipment and machinery. Pierre had been in the middle of a particle collision experiment when this fracas occurred. Lying on the floor, the machinery whirred and roared in Angelo's confused ears. He blinked away some of the red and saw the soft glow of the banks of computers in the room for the first time.

It was difficult to breathe. The shock had triggered an acute asthma attack. Angelo tried to gulp down air, but only succeeded in sucking blood from the wounds on his face into his lungs. He was drowning in a room full of air. As his life slowly slipped away, he saw Jill's beautiful face. He reached out to touch it. He wanted to hold on to her, to her love, for the last time. It was then that he remembered and in his half-alive state, memory took on the consistency of a dreamlike reality.

Jill was suddenly here in the lab with him. She seemed semi-solid and wispy, like a ghost. Angelo reached out to her. He tried to hold on to her, but it was like grasping air. Jill laughed shrilly and stepped just out of his reach. She held her arms out to him. He reached for her, but he could not touch her. Her voice wafted up to him from the red haze.

"Angelo," she called in a soft sing-song tone that seemed more dream than reality. "Angelo my love, don't die yet. I have something to tell you."

"Jill," Angelo gasped, sputtering blood all over the computer screens. "Jill, I love you."

"Oh Angelo," the ghostly Jill said, "You shouldn't love me. I don't deserve your love."

"Oh Jill, how can you say that? I love you," Angelo moaned.

"You know why, Angelo. You know my love is untrue," ghost Jill sighed.

Angelo lifted his head with an effort. He saw the ghostly form of Jill through a dull, red haze. She wore a floaty white nightgown that skimmed delicately over her protruding, round belly.
"Oh Jill," Angelo sobbed. "Oh Jill."

He gasped for air and struggled upright. He managed to get onto his unsteady feet and stumbled forward. He fell, gasping, beside the particle collider.

"What is life, that we should grasp on to it; clutch it with all our might, hold on, completely unwilling to let go?" he screamed.

Pierre dropped the handset and rushed over towards him. "No, get away from there!" Pierre shouted. "You can't be that close to the particle collider!"

"Particles," Angelo mumbled, spraying bubbles of blood from his half-open lips as he did so. Life, energy, matter, antimatter. Vanity.

He suddenly pulled himself upright and leaned on the operator console. His weight depressed the button controlling the particle chamber and it slid open silently, revealing a dark cavern pulsating with the microscopic particles of radioactive experimental material.

“Do emotions contain antimatter?” Angelo raved. “Does the negative energy heaped on one man throughout the course of a lifetime matter? What happens if this energy is released at the moment of death?”

His voice faltered as it petered down to a whisper.

“Does anything actually matter? Let’s see.”

He stepped into the void. There was surprisingly little noise as the door slid closed behind him and the particle collider switched on.

“Noooooooo!!!!!” Pierre screamed. His scream was silenced by an all-encompassing orange-red flash.

Minutes, seconds, nanoseconds, years or eons later, Angelo awoke in the midst of the primordial orange-red soup. There was no time left in the universe. Nothing mattered, yet everything was matter.

He was alone. He was immortal. He was matter.

www.ingramcontent.com/pod-product-compliance
Ingram Content Group UK Ltd.
Pitfield, Milton Keynes, MK11 3LW, UK
UKHW020216250726
13967UKWH00001B/28

9 781300 067887